Young Cousins Mysteries™
The Giant Chicken Mystery

P9-CCT-301

by Elspeth Campbell Murphy

Illustrated by Nancy Munger

Timothy   Sarah-Jane   Titus

The Lord has made both these things:
Ears that can hear and eyes that can see.

Proverbs 20:12

The Giant Chicken Mystery
Copyright © 2002
Elspeth Campbell Murphy

Cover and story illustrations by Nancy Munger
Cover design by Jennifer Parker

Young Cousins Mysteries is a trademark of Elspeth Campbell Murphy.

Scripture quotation is from the *International Children's Bible, New Century Version,*
copyright © 1986, 1988 by Word Publishing, Dallas, Texas 75039.
Used by permission.

Published by Bethany House Publishers
A Ministry of Bethany Fellowship International
11400 Hampshire Avenue South
Bloomington, Minnesota 55438
www.bethanyhouse.com

Printed in China.

Library of Congress Catalog-in-Publication Data

CIP data applied for

ISBN 0-7642-2496-4

Contents

Chapter One
The Chicken Riddle

Sarah-Jane Cooper sat with her cousins Timothy and Titus on a cute little bench.

The cute little bench sat in front of some cute little stores.

Timothy and Titus did not like cute little stores.

They especially did not like cute little fabric stores.

And Mrs. Cooper had just gone into Buttons 'n Bows.

So the cousins decided to wait outside.

They knew it would be a l-o-n-g wait.

Fortunately, Mrs. Cooper had given them money for Roxie's Finest Fudge.

Also fortunately, Sarah-Jane had a gift certificate for Books, Books, Books.

The certificate came from a summer reading program.

It was still early in the summer.

But Sarah-Jane had already read enough to get a prize.

Sarah-Jane was an excellent reader.

And everyone said she had *quite* an imagination!

Timothy and Titus helped her pick out a book of riddles.

So they had fudge and riddles. They were all set to wait outside on the cute little bench.

"OK. Here's one," said Sarah-Jane. "Why did the chicken cross the road?"

"To get to the other side," said Timothy and Titus together.

"You've heard that one," said Sarah-Jane.

"Yup," said Timothy and Titus together.

Sarah-Jane handed them the book.

"OK," she said. "You find one."

Sarah-Jane leaned back and closed her eyes.

When she opened her eyes,
she saw a giant chicken crossing the road.

Sarah-Jane turned to her cousins.

"You guys! Look! Look!
A giant chicken crossing the road!"

"A *what*?" said Timothy and Titus.

"A *giant chicken*!" cried Sarah-Jane.
"Look!"

But when she turned back around,
the chicken was gone.

Chapter Two
The Chicken Feather

"A giant chicken," said Timothy.

"Crossing the road," said Titus.

"Yes!" cried Sarah-Jane. "Yes! Yes! Yes! It was right over there!"

Timothy and Titus looked to where she was pointing. There was no giant chicken.

"Are you sure you didn't imagine it?" asked Timothy.

"No! I most certainly did not imagine it!" said Sarah-Jane.

She didn't stamp her foot, but she came close.

"Maybe you dreamed it," suggested
Titus. "Maybe you dozed off for a
minute. And maybe you dreamed it
because we were just talking about the
chicken joke."

"No! I most certainly did not
dream it," said Sarah-Jane.

This time she did stamp her foot.

"Why don't you two believe me?" she asked. "After all, you guys once saw a gorilla on my front porch."

"That's different," said Timothy. "There really was a gorilla on your front porch."

"Well," said Sarah-Jane. "There really was a giant chicken crossing the road."

Suddenly, something on the sidewalk caught her eye.

She ran over and picked it up.

"Aha!" she cried. "What do you call this?"

"It's a feather," said Titus.

"But it's not white," said Timothy. "How can it be from a chicken if it's not white?"

"Not *all* chickens are white," said Sarah-Jane. "Some are reddish brown. Like the chicken *I* saw. Like this feather."

"Right," said Titus. "It's like that story of the Little Red Hen, who planted wheat and baked bread. I guess that's how they came up with the name of that bakery over there."

The cousins looked at the cute little bakery in the row of other cute little stores.

It was called The Little Red Hen.

They looked at one another.

It didn't hurt to ask. . . .

Chapter Three
The Missing Chicken

The bell jangled over the door as the cousins came in.

The owner, Mrs. White, looked up and smiled. "Hello, my darlings! What can I do for you?"

Sarah-Jane felt a little silly asking about a giant chicken.

But sometimes you're so curious, you can live with feeling silly.

"Um . . . Mrs. White . . ." began Sarah-Jane. "You wouldn't happen to know anything about a giant chicken, would you?"

To their surprise, Mrs. White just beamed at them.

"Of course, sweetheart! It's my latest idea! I hired someone to dress up like the Little Red Hen.

"The Little Red Hen will stand outside the bakery and hand out free samples.

"People who taste the samples will come into the bakery to buy more."

The cousins agreed that this was
a good idea.

But it didn't explain why Sarah-Jane
had seen the chicken crossing the road.

Just then the bell over the door
jangled.

"Ah! Here is my chicken now!" said
Mrs. White.

The cousins turned to see their friend Liz.

The last time they had seen her, she was wearing a gorilla costume and singing "Happy Birthday to You."

She was not wearing a costume now.

Something didn't make sense. . . .

"Go and get changed, dear," Mrs. White told her. "The costume is in the back room."

Liz was back in a minute.

"I can't find the costume," she said.

Mrs. White hurried back to see for herself.

She was back in a minute.

"The costume is gone!" she said.

Timothy said, "Someone went into the back room and took the costume."

"And probably sneaked out the back door," said Sarah-Jane.

"It sounds like an inside job," said Titus.

"Yes," said Mrs. White. "It certainly does!"

Chapter Four
The Surprised Chicken

Mrs. White said to her assistant, "Suzie, did my nephew George come by today?"

"Yes," said Suzie. "He went in the back room. But I didn't see him leave."

"Hmmm . . ." said Mrs. White.

The cousins could guess what she was thinking.

"Did your nephew dress up like a chicken?" asked Timothy. *Why?*

"Who knows why that boy does anything?" said Mrs. White. "He's always clowning around!"

Sarah-Jane showed Mrs. White and Liz the feather.

She told about seeing the giant chicken crossing the road.

Titus said, "But *why* did the chicken cross the road? What's on the other side?"

They all went to the window to see.

Across the street was the community center with a sign in the window.

The sign said *Summer Driver's Education Classes Begin Today.*

"Is George taking driver's ed?" asked Titus. "In a *chicken costume?*"

"No," said Mrs. White. "George already has his license. But his friends don't. Come with me."

The bell over the door jangled loudly as Mrs. White marched out.

Timothy, Titus, Sarah-Jane, and Liz trotted along behind her.

Mrs. White led them across the street and around behind the community center.

And that's where they saw the giant chicken.

He was popping up and down in front of the classroom windows.

It was pretty funny.

It must have looked *really* funny to the kids who were inside the classroom . . . as long as the teacher didn't see!

"George!" said Mrs. White sternly.
"That is *not* funny!"

The cousins could tell she was trying
very hard not to laugh.

"Uh-oh," said the chicken.

Chapter Five
The Chicken Tale

At long last, Mrs. Cooper came out of the fabric store.

She found the three cousins sitting on the cute little bench in front of the cute little stores.

They were reading a riddle book and eating giant cookies.

"Where did you get those great-looking cookies?" she asked them.

"Mrs. White gave them to us," said Timothy.

"For free," said Titus.

"Oh!" said Mrs. Cooper. "Well, that was nice of her. . . ."

"It was to say thank-you," explained Sarah-Jane. "We helped her find her giant chicken."

"That chicken?" asked Sarah-Jane's mother.

She pointed to the chicken handing out samples in front of the bakery.

"No," said Sarah-Jane. "That's Liz. George is the chicken we found."

"Liz is getting paid," said Titus. "But George has to do some work for free, because he was clowning around."

Timothy said, "Liz is really nice. But as chickens go, I think George is funnier."

Sarah-Jane and Titus nodded.
They had to agree with that.

"Uh . . . okaaay . . ." said Mrs. Cooper.

Then Mrs. Cooper noticed the riddle book.

"Speaking of chickens, here's a riddle. Why did the chicken cross the road?"

The cousins just looked at one another and grinned.

"You've heard that one," said Mrs. Cooper.

"Yup," said Sarah-Jane.

The End